RORY
and his
Christmas Surprise

Author: Andrew Wolffe   Illustrator: Tom Cole

Text and illustrations copyright © Keppel Publishing, 2003.
The Rory Stories is a Registered Trademark of Keppel Publishing.
This edition published 2003.   ISBN: 0 9534949 9 3

A CIP catalogue record for this book is available from the British Library.

Printed in Singapore

Keppel Publishing Ltd.
The Grey House, Kenbridge Road,
New Galloway, DG7 3RP, Scotland.

It was Christmas Eve in Sandy Bay and the snow was falling fast. Rory and Scruff McDuff were cosy at home helping Rory's Mum to hang the last of the decorations on the Christmas tree that stretched up high above them.

When the angel was safely on top of the tree it was time for Rory's favourite part.

"Three, two, one...," Rory gave the count down, then his Mum clicked on the switch and countless little lights flashed on together and bathed the Christmas tree in bright glowing red.

"There's the doorbell," Rory's Mum
said as she stepped back to admire the tree.
"Maybe it's Santa?" Rory asked
hopefully.
"Santa comes when everyone's fast
asleep," Rory's Mum gently reminded
him as she walked towards the door.
"It's probably Sid the Sweep
to clean our chimney."

The chimney in Rory's house is swept every Christmas Eve in honour of Santa's visit. This year Rory's Mum thought something was blocking the chimney, so Sid the Sweep chose his longest, bushiest brush and set to work.

"Look what I've found," exclaimed Sid the Sweep, holding up a sooty wellington boot.

"I wonder who it belongs to?" asked Rory.

"And how it got there?" added Rory's Mum.

"It wasn't me Mum." Rory answered quickly. "And Scruff McDuff only hides bones."

Mystified by the strange discovery, Rory and Scruff McDuff decided to check the other wellingtons in the house to see if one was missing.

There were small boots, big boots, green boots, red boots, blue boots and boots old and new.

But they couldn't find a boot to match the one that Sid the Sweep had found.

"I don't know, Scruff McDuff," Rory said in bewilderment. "Perhaps it belongs to Uncle Jack; it looks like a fisherman's wellington. Do you think it's his?"

"No," Rory continued with certainty. "It must belong to someone else, someone who goes down chimneys, someone like..."

Suddenly Rory knew exactly who the wellington belonged to.

"...Santa Claus!" Rory shouted in delight. "It must belong to Santa. Let's put it where he can find it when he comes tonight with our presents."

"Scruff McDuff's got the right idea," Rory's Dad said with a smile as he finished hanging up Rory's Christmas stocking later that evening. "Time you were fast asleep too, Rory. Santa might not deliver your Christmas presents if you aren't tucked up in bed."

Like all children on Christmas Eve, Rory was trying to be good. He had almost fallen asleep when he heard an unusual sound. He quickly jumped out of bed, pulled on his trousers and jumper over his pyjamas and tip-toed over to Scruff McDuff.

"Psst, wake up," Rory whispered urgently. "I heard Santa's sleigh bells and I think he's landed on our roof. We'd better be quiet as mice," he added before they set off down the stairs.

Rory was bursting with excitement at the thought of seeing Santa Claus. But an even more amazing sight greeted the little chums as they peered round the door of the living room.

"Look! Santa's only wearing one wellington," Rory exclaimed, just as the excitement got too much for Scruff McDuff and he gave a little yelp.

"I see you found the wellington that I lost last year, Rory," Santa said with a smile.

"Your toes must be very cold if you haven't been wearing one since then," Rory replied with concern.

"Ho, Ho, Ho," laughed Santa. "No, No, No. I lost the one from this foot only a few villages ago. In a very tricky chimney, I might add."

"I'm always losing wellingtons," Santa sighed as he sat down on the sofa. "Fortunately, Mrs Claus keeps plenty of spares for me back at the North Pole.

"I'll just slip this one on meantime.
Thank you for the milk and biscuits, but I've
had plenty already," Santa added, patting his
tummy. "You and Scruff McDuff tuck in.
Now, I wonder if you can help me?"

Just as Rory had heard, Santa's sleigh and reindeer were parked on Rory's roof. There weren't many presents left in the sack because Santa had only one more house to visit.

"I've been all over Sandy Bay but I can't find the harbourmaster's house," Santa explained. "It doesn't seem to be beside the harbour. Will you and Scruff McDuff show me where it is?"

No sooner had Rory nodded his
head in agreement than he and Scruff McDuff
were being whisked through the cold night air.
"The harbourmaster and his family live out
beyond Sandy Bay lighthouse," Rory informed
Santa as the reindeer galloped across the sky.

"Well done, Rory," Santa said with a smile when the sleigh slid to a halt outside the harbourmaster's house. "Now everyone will have their presents on Christmas morning."

In less time than it takes for a snowflake to melt on the palm of your hand, Rory and Scruff McDuff were back outside their house.

"Straight to bed you two," Santa Claus said kindly. "And no peeping in your Christmas stockings until morning."

"We won't, Santa," Rory promised as he waved goodbye.

And you won't either, will you?